Willimena
and the
Cookie Money

By Valerie Wilson Wesley

SCHOLASTIC INC.
New York Toronto London Auckland Sydney
Mexico City New Delhi Hong Kong Buenos Aires

ISBN 0-439-35772-1

Copyright © 2000 by Valerie Wilson Wesley.
Cover illustration copyright © 2001 by Scott Nash.
All rights reserved.
Published by Scholastic Inc., 555 Broadway, New York, NY 10012,
by arrangement with Hyperion Books for Children, an imprint of
Disney Children's Book Group, LLC.
SCHOLASTIC and associated logos are trademarks and/or
registered trademarks of Scholastic Inc.

12 11 10 9 8 7 6 5 4 3 2 1   1 2 3 4 5 6/0

Printed in the U.S.A.   40

First Scholastic printing, October 2001

The text of this book is set in 14-point New Century Schoolbook.

For the kids in Ms. Rice's class and all
of the children who attend the
Whitney E. Houston Academy

Got You Back!

The cookie money was gone! Well, most of it, anyway. Three weeks ago, I had $25.75. I earned it by selling Girl Scout cookies. I kept it in the purple tin box where I keep my birthday money. Dollar by dollar, quarter by quarter, dime by dime, I spent twenty dollars of it. It was money that really didn't belong to me, and there was only $5.75 left. I, Willimena Thomas, seven years old, was a thief.

I was supposed to give the money to

Mrs. Jones, our troop leader, on the last day of Brownies. But I got a sore throat and couldn't go to the meeting. The next week my mom went back to work and couldn't drive me. Then my dad started graduate school, and our baby-sitter, Mrs. Cotton, doesn't drive. Then Mrs. Jones went out of town. Then the Brownies stopped meeting for the summer. Yesterday, Mrs. Jones called my mom and told her to bring the money to her house next Monday. That's a week from today. I don't know what I'm going to do.

"Willie! Come down and get your pan-cakes before they get cold," my mom yelled from the kitchen. Everybody calls me Willie, which is short for Willimena.

"Okay," I yelled back. But I knew the pancakes wouldn't go down. My throat was too tight. I shoved the purple tin box into my desk drawer as far back as I could push it. I slipped on my red socks—my good-luck socks—tied my sneakers, and went downstairs. I didn't want anybody to know I was worried, so I pulled my lips into a grin. I sat down at the kitchen table across from Tina, my big sister.

"Mornin', stupid," Tina said. I breathed a sigh of relief. Tina said "Mornin', stupid" almost every morning. My secret was safe.

"Tina, don't start the day calling Willie names." My mom gave Tina a warning look. Tina looked away and poured syrup on her pancakes. She drew a squiggly line with the syrup and then printed her name across her stack of pancakes. She dotted the "i" in "Tina" with a smiley face. She always does that whenever we have pancakes. My mom poured some coffee into her cup. She took a sip, looked at the clock, and gasped.

"Oh, my! Look at the time!" she said. My mom started working at a newspaper three weeks ago. She's always in a rush. She always gets home late. I hardly have time to talk to her anymore. I really miss her. The good thing about her working is that we always know what's going to be on the front page of the newspaper. The bad thing is Mrs. Cotton, our baby-sitter.

Mom kissed me and Tina before she headed out the door. "Tell Mrs. Cotton that there's tuna fish for lunch and tell your dad to buy some food for Doofus Doolittle," she said. Doofus Doolittle is our cat. His fur is black, and he has a pointed face and big golden eyes. He's the cutest cat I've ever seen.

I watched my mom as she got in her car and pulled out of the driveway. I spread some butter on my pancakes, picked up the syrup bottle, and held it over my pancakes. Ten dinky drops dripped out. I glared at Tina. She picked up a forkful of pancakes and nibbled on them. Syrup dripped off her fork onto her plate.

"Pig!" I said. Just my luck, my dad was coming down the stairs and heard me.

"Willimena!" Dad wrinkled up his face into a frown. "I don't want to hear any name-calling this morning."

"But she called me stupid, and you said not to call me that anymore," I said. Tina rolled her eyes.

"Tina!" He still had a frown on his face "I've told you about that. Nobody is stupid in this family. I don't want to hear you say that word again." He poured some water in a kettle to make himself a cup of peppermint tea.

"But she always says mean things to me," Tina said.

"But she always starts it," I said.

"That's not true. Willie is such a baby!"

"Tina, you're my big girl. You should know better. It's up to you to set a good example," my dad said.

"But that's not fair! She always gets

5

away with everything just because she's younger than me." Tina banged her fork down on her plate with a frown.

"No, I don't!"

"Yes, you do!"

"You two!" My dad shook his head. "You know who you two are?"

Tina and I started to laugh. We always did whenever my father asked that question because we knew what the answer was.

"You two are the Sisters Umoja!" he said. *Umoja* means "unity" in Swahili, which means that we are supposed to be united and get along. My dad calls us that because Tina and I fight all the time. It's his idea of a joke. Doofus Doolittle came over and rubbed against my dad's leg, and he bent down to pat him. My dad had to bend a long way down because he's very tall.

"Morning, Mr. D.," he said to our cat.

Mr. D. is my dad's name for Doofus Doolittle.

"Mom said to not to forget to buy Doofus some food. He's almost out," Tina said.

"Thanks for remembering, Big Girl," my dad said. "Big Girl" is my dad's nickname for Tina. Sometimes he calls me Little One. I'm not crazy about that. He patted Tina on her head, and she smiled up at him. I knew he was was trying to let her know that he wasn't mad at her even though he'd warned her about calling me names. My dad is nice like that.

The doorbell rang, and my dad went to answer it. Tina rolled her eyes and I poked out my mouth. We knew who it was. It was Mrs. Cotton. The one thing Tina and I are united about is Mrs. Cotton.

"Good morning, Mr. Thomas and Little Thomases," Mrs. Cotton said. Every morning she says the same thing. It gets on my nerves.

"Good morning, Mrs. Cotton," Tina and I said together.

"Well, Mrs. Cotton. How are you doing this morning?" my father asked her.

"Oh, not well, Mr. Thomas, not well at all!"

"Oh, dear. What's wrong?" my dad asked. Mrs. Cotton sank into a chair. She took off her yellow straw hat with gray flowers on it and put it on the table—right next to my pancakes. Then she tugged on her wig to straighten it. Mrs. Cotton's wig is red, but her real hair is gray. You can see it whenever she moves her wig.

"I hate to trouble you with my troubles, Mr. Thomas," she said. Mrs. Cotton says that every morning, too.

"Has your rheumatism been bothering you again?" my dad asked. We could tell he was really worried about her.

"Well, that's just one thing," Mrs. Cotton said. She rubbed her knee. Then she started to cough. "I'm getting a cold, too. I was up late last night sniffling, sneezing, and carrying on like a fool." She patted the side of her cheek. "Then my tooth got to hurting when I got up this morning. I don't know what I'm going to do about these bad teeth of mine. And I nearly fell on the sidewalk on the way up to your house. Some careless somebody left a skateboard right in the middle of the sidewalk!" She glanced at me and Tina.

"Not us!" we said together.

"Why don't you rest your feet awhile, and I'll fix you a nice cup of peppermint tea," my dad said, as he poured Mrs. Cotton a cup of tea.

"You're so kind, Mr. Thomas, so very kind," she said. "Little Thomases, you are so lucky to have a father as kind as Mr. Thomas."

"Thank you, Mrs. Cotton." We said that together, too.

Suddenly Tina started to giggle. She does that sometimes. She giggled so hard I didn't think she could stop. Then I started to giggle because Tina looked so funny with her hand covering her mouth. When Mrs. Cotton bent over to rub her knee, Tina giggled even louder. Then I started. We couldn't stop. Our dad gave us a warning look.

"Time for me to go," he said. "Now I want you two to behave yourselves."

"We will," we both said. Maybe we *were* the Sisters Umoja.

But then I remembered there was no syrup left. "Can you get some syrup off the shelf before you leave?" I asked my dad. It was on the top of the pantry, and I knew that Mrs. Cotton, with her bad knee, wouldn't want to climb up on a stool to get it.

"Sure, sugar," my dad said. He is the only one in our family who is tall enough to get things off the top shelf of the pantry. He took some cans of beans and a jar of apple-sauce off the shelf and put them on the counter. Then he stood on his toes and felt the back of the shelf with his hand. He shook his head.

"I don't think we have any more, Willie. I guess you'll have to have honey," he said. He took down a jar of honey with a smiling bee on the label and put it on the table in front of me. I don't like honey on pancakes. They don't taste the same. I threw Tina a mean look.

"You hogged all the syrup!" I said.

"Early bird gets the worm," Tina said. She took another bite of her pancakes.

"But that's unfair!" I wailed. "You can be so mean, Tina!"

"Well, you used up all the chocolate syrup yesterday and that was mean!" Tina said.

"No, I didn't!"

"Yes, you did. And you didn't give me the remote to the TV last night. I'm getting you back for that, too!" Tina added.

"But you always have it!" I wailed back.

"Girls, stop this right now! Stop it!" my father said. He doesn't usually yell at us, but he did now. I looked down at my pancakes and then at Tina. A drop of syrup dribbled down the front of her blouse.

"I'm going to get you back for this," I said. I felt like I was going to cry.

"'I'm going to get you back for this,'" Tina said. She was imitating me. The only thing that makes me madder than when Tina calls me a crybaby is when she imitates me.

"No more!" my dad said. We knew that he meant it.

"Tsk, tsk, tsk," Mrs. Cotton said and shook her finger at us. "Little Thomases, you *must* act like nice little ladies! You must behave."

I spread some honey on my pancakes. It was so thick I tore a hole through the top pancake. I took a bite. I gave Tina the hardest kick I could under the table. I knew it was a terrible thing to do, but I did it anyway.

"Ouch!" Tina screamed.

"Got you back!" I whispered. I pulled my chair out of reach of her foot. I took another bite of my pancake. It didn't taste as bad as the first one. Tina narrowed her eyes and glared at me.

"Dad," she said as my father opened the door to leave.

"Yeah, Big Girl."

"Did Mom tell you that Mrs. Jones called?"

The pancake with the honey stuck to the top of my mouth.

"What did she want?"

"She wants you or Mom to bring over Willie's cookie money next Monday. All twenty-five dollars and seventy-five cents of it."

I took a big gulp of orange juice.

"Then one of us will take it to her," my dad said.

"All twenty-five dollars and seventy-five cents?"

"Sure. Is that how much money you earned, Willie?"

I couldn't say anything. I couldn't even look my dad in the eye. I felt worse than I had ever felt in my life.

Tina dabbed a piece of pancake into the pool of syrup on her plate. "Got you back!" she whispered.

Big Sisters

You probably think my big sister Tina runs a close second to the meanest monster in my scariest nightmares. But Tina is nice most of the time. Well, some of the time. Okay, maybe a couple of days a month.

When I told Amber, who lives next door, everything that had happened, she shook her head. Amber is my best friend. She has an older sister, too. Her sister's name is Lydia, and she's the same age as Tina. Amber understands what big sisters are like.

"That's bad news, Willie, real bad news," Amber said. We were sitting on her back porch playing checkers, which is our favorite game. We play it every day. Amber jumped one of my pieces and moved to the king's row. "How did Tina find out the money was gone?"

"She was probably snooping around my things like she always does," I said. I got mad just thinking about it. I double-jumped Amber. "King me!" I said. It was the best thing that had happened to me so far that day.

"Good move!" Amber nodded with approval and plopped a checker on top of mine. Amber is usually a good sport. The only time she's not is when she's playing with her sister, Lydia. Then she goes for blood. "If I were a big sister, I'd never be mean the way Lydia and Tina are to us," she said.

"If I had a younger sister, I'd always let

her have the syrup and the ice cream first, and I'd give her the remote when she asked for it," I said.

"Yeah. I'd never make up things to fool my little sister. Remember that time Lydia told me I was adopted?" Amber asked.

"How could I forget something like that?" I said.

It was only three years ago. Amber and I were four, young enough to believe the dumb things our sisters told us. Lydia told Amber she had proof that she was adopted. She took out the family photo album and counted all the pictures of herself when she was a baby. Then she counted all the pictures of Amber. There were ten times more pictures of her than of Amber. The only baby picture the Washingtons had of Amber was taken when she was a year old. Lydia said that was proof that Amber had been a year old when she came to live with them. Lydia claimed that she remembered the day that Amber came. She said a man in a green SUV had dropped Amber off on the front stoop. Finally, Mrs. Washington set Amber straight and made Lydia apologize. But Amber never forgot it.

"Remember the time Tina hid Penguin behind the washing machine in the basement and told me that my mom had given him to the Salvation Army?" I said. Penguin is my favorite stuffed animal. I've had him since I was a baby. I cried for hours when I thought he was gone. Finally my mom made Tina give him back. That happened two years ago.

"That was terrible!" Amber said with a sigh. "Poor Penguin! It still makes me sad when I think of his little stuffed body stuck behind the washing machine." Amber double-jumped me, and I put a checker on her piece without saying anything.

"Remember the time Lydia broke Mom's

pearl necklace and put the pearls on my bed?" Amber asked.

"Yeah," I said. The more we remembered how mean our big sisters had been to us, the madder we both got. We played checkers in silence, slapping down our pieces on the board.

"But sometimes Tina is nice," I said after a while.

"Sometimes Lydia is, too," Amber added. "Like last week, when we watched that scary show on TV. I was real frightened, and Lydia let me sleep in her bed."

"Remember last Halloween?" I said.

"That was bad news, real bad news." Amber shook her head as she remembered.

It *had* been very bad news until Tina saved the day.

My dad had taken me, Amber, Lydia, and Tina trick-or-treating. My trick-or-treat bag was made out of orange and black paper. It started to rain, and my bag tore, but I didn't know it until I got home. Then it was too late. All of my candy had fallen out. I can still remember the sinking feeling in my stomach.

"Tina gave me *half* of her candy! Half of it!" I said. Even now I had a hard time believing it.

"That was *sooo* nice of Tina," Amber said. "That was the nicest thing I ever heard of anybody's sister doing. She even gave you half of her Almond Joys!" Tales of Tina's generosity had spread up and down our street. Kids still talked about it.

"Tina can really be nice when she wants to. Just like an older sister should be," I said, and Amber agreed. I thought some more about how nice my big sister could be sometimes. Then I said, "Maybe I shouldn't be mad at Tina about the cookie money. If it hadn't been for Tina I wouldn't have made any money at all."

"You're right about that," Amber said as

she moved a piece and then took it back. Tina, my sometimes mean big sister, had helped me become a super salesgirl.

I was *really* scared the day that Mrs. Jones told our troop we were going to sell Girl Scout cookies. I didn't think anybody would buy them from me. I was afraid that I would ring the doorbell and nobody would answer. I was scared I wouldn't know what to say. I was sure I'd be the only Brownie in the troop who wouldn't sell any cookies.

But Tina came to the rescue. She helped me develop confidence. She told me what to say. She'd even stood at my side when I made my first sale.

Every night after we took our baths and brushed our teeth, Tina and I rehearsed. Tina would get into the closet and close the door behind her. I'd knock, and she would pretend to be a mean customer.

"Can I help you, little girl?" she would ask in a gruff voice.

She would squeeze her face into a tight ball and poke out her lips. She would narrow her eyes. With all the lights out, she really did look like somebody else.

"Smile, Willie. Always smile," Tina said. "No matter how mean somebody acts, smile. Act like you're doing something special. Like you're doing a commercial on TV. Let's try it again."

We rehearsed about five times that first night until my mom told us to go to bed. After two or three nights of rehearsal, Tina decided that I knew what I was doing. I was ready for the big time. When it was time to sell my first box of cookies, Tina was there to help me out.

"Ring the doorbell. And whatever you do, don't just stand there looking dumb!" she said. "And remember what I told you about smiling. If you forget, I'm going to kick you on the ankle!"

But I didn't forget. Tina told me to start out with somebody easy. I chose Mrs. Ross. She is the nicest lady on our street. She always gives us good candy for Halloween—full-size candy bars, real packs of gum—no cheap stuff. Mrs. Ross bought three boxes of cookies. I was on my way. By the time it got dark, I'd worked my way up to Mrs. Pyle. Everybody on our street calls her Pyle the Pill. Mrs. Pyle never smiles. She always yells at us when we play in front of her house. Once she squirted Doofus with her hose. Mrs. Pyle bought two boxes of cookies. I couldn't believe it!

The next day, Tina and I crossed Chestnut Avenue, and I sold cookies over there. I had so many cookie orders I could barely write them all down. I was a success. A super-salesgirl! The next week was better than the first. By the end of the week I'd made fifty dollars. I took it to my troop meeting and turned it in. Mrs. Jones said that I had sold more cookies than anybody else. And it had all been because of Tina. The third week, I earned $25.75. That was when my troubles began.

"Sometimes big sisters will look out for you when nobody else will," Amber said. "Lydia is nice sometimes, too. Sometimes she even lets me beat her at checkers."

"For real?" I jumped one of Amber's pieces.

Amber looked surprised. "Didn't see that," she said. I smiled. If she had, I wouldn't have been able to do it.

"You never told me what happened to the money," Amber said as we started another game. "Twenty dollars doesn't just disappear."

"I spent it," I said.

"But what did you spend it on?" Amber asked.

Before I could say anything, Lana and

Lena, the twins who live at the end of our street, ran up on the porch. Amber didn't know it, but the answer to her question had just plopped down next to her.

Lena and Lana

Lena and Lana are twins. They look exactly alike. They both have braids. They wear the same kind of sneakers—red and white with blue shoestrings. They both have teeth missing in the same spot. They talk the same way—very fast. The only way I can tell them apart is when they chew gum. Lana chews gum slowly, like a regular person. Lena cracks it. I've never heard anybody crack gum like Lena can. It snaps and crackles. It pops and spits. It bangs inside her mouth like a firecracker. It's the greatest noise I've ever heard. I've tried to do it, but I can't. Gum just lumps in my mouth and doesn't go anywhere.

Lena and Lana have lived on our street for only about three weeks, with their aunt, Miss Wynn. But I feel like I've known them forever. They're new kids, but they don't act that way. Before they came, Miss Wynn lived by herself. Her house is very old. It's painted a dull color of gray. The green shutters on the windows are loose, and hang to the side. The grass in front of the house is very long. Before Lena and Lana moved in, Tina and Lydia used to tell me and Amber that her house was haunted. We believed them. A lot of kids on our street wouldn't ring Miss Wynn's bell on Halloween.

But that's all changed now. Everybody knows the house is okay because Lena and Lana live there. I'll never forget the first day I saw them. They were walking down the street dressed exactly alike. They both had on red shorts and white-and-red shirts. They both wore sunglasses shaped like stars. They acted like they had lived on our block all their lives.

Lana was bouncing a yo-yo. I've never seen anybody bounce a yo-yo like Lana does. She reels it in and out and makes it do whatever she wants. Lena was shuffling a deck of cards. When they joined Amber and me on the porch, Lana was bouncing the same yo-yo and Lena was playing with the same deck of cards.

"Anybody want to play some cards?" Lena asked. She loves to play cards. She is the best card player I've ever seen. She plays war and twenty-one like a pro. She even knows how to play poker. When she doesn't have anybody to play with she plays solitaire. She always wins. I've never seen anything like it.

Lana watched her sister from the corner of her eye. "Put those cards away, Lena. Nobody's going to play with you. Everybody knows you—"

"I don't cheat!" Lena said. She popped her gum loud.

"Yes, you—" Lana whirled out her yo-yo and reeled it back in.

"No, I don't and I wasn't—" Lena snapped her cards down on the stair.

"I don't care if you were talking to me or not!"

Lena and Lana always knew what the other one was getting ready to say. One of them would say something. Then the other one would finish her sentence for her. They were funny when they really got going. Amber and I could listen to them for hours.

"Did you get the key from—" started Lana.

"Aunt Wynn gave it to—" finished Lena.

"Don't say—" said Lana.

29

"But she left it with—" started Lena.

"But that was last—"

"Don't say Thursday because—"

"It wasn't Thursday, it was—"

"Well, we agree on something!" Lena said, rolling her eyes.

"Well, you had it last—" said Lana.

"No, you—"

Lana and Lena argued back and forth, beginning and finishing each other's sentences for the next five minutes. Then they sat together in the same big chair. They crossed their legs in the same direction. Lana put down her yo-yo. Lena put down her deck of cards.

"So who has the key?" Amber asked them.

"Nobody!" Lena and Lana said together. "We're locked out again."

We all laughed.

Miss. Wynn, Lena and Lana's aunt, leaves for work early in the morning. One of them, Amber and I were never sure who, was supposed to get the key from her before she left. Somebody, we never knew who, always forgot to do it.

"That's bad news, real bad news!" said Amber.

"So why doesn't your aunt leave the key in a secret place?" I asked.

Lena and Lana shrugged, moving their shoulders in the very same way.

"So what are you going to do for lunch?" It was just about time for lunch, and I was starting to get hungry. Lana and Lena looked at each other and shrugged. The looks on both of their faces told me the answer.

Just then, Mrs. Cotton came walking down the street.

"Willie, Willie, Willie!" she called out. She always says my name three times when she looks for me on my block. It gets on my nerves. She spotted me sitting on

Amber's porch, and she came over toward us.

"Thank goodness, I found one little Thomas. Where is the other little Thomas?" I didn't say anything. I just frowned. That "little Thomas" business was bad enough at home. I couldn't stand it out here where everybody could hear it.

"In her room," I said, "where she's been all day." I didn't mean to sound fresh, but I could tell by Mrs. Cotton's face that I did. I hoped she wouldn't say anything about acting like a nice little lady in front of Amber.

"Well, it's time you came home too. It's almost time for lunch," Mrs. Cotton said, and then turned to go.

I got up to leave. Lena and Lana both sighed together. The same sound. The same length. It sounded as if it were coming from the very same mouth.

"Would you-all like to come to my

house and have lunch?" I asked them.

"Sure, Willie, thanks!" they said together.

We said good-bye to Amber and headed back to my house to get something to eat.

Lunch

The three of us came into my kitchen and sat down at the table. There were two tuna-fish sandwich halves left on the plate. They had been made with the ends of the loaf. One slice was white, the other was brown. Neither had a crust. Tuna fish spilled from the sides of both.

Tina had taken the two good halves and was munching away. The ketchup jar was next to her juice. Tina liked ketchup on her tuna-fish sandwich. She put huge dots of ketchup on her plate. Then she dipped the end of her sandwich into the ketchup. Then she ate it. Tina is probably the only person in the world who likes ketchup and tuna fish. I picked up one of the ugly sandwiches. I watched Tina eat her tuna-and-ketchup sandwich. I put my sandwich back on the plate. I didn't feel like eating.

"Can I—?" Lana asked me.

"Have your sandwich?" added Lena.

"I asked first," Lana said.

"We'll share!" said Lena.

Lena and Lana each took half of the sandwich that was left and quickly ate it. I knew they must really be hungry. Anyone who could eat an ugly sandwich like that sitting across from Tina and her ketchup-and-tuna-fish feast had to be.

"Want the other one?" I asked.

"Sure!" they said together. "Thanks, Willie!"

That was when Mrs. Cotton came into the kitchen.

"Please put that sandwich back!" she said to Lena. We all turned around to look at her in surprise. Even Tina put down the ketchup bottle. "Young lady, please put that down. That last sandwich belongs to Willimena," Mrs. Cotton said.

"But I don't want it!" I said. "I want Lena and Lana to have it."

"Mrs. Thomas made those sandwiches for the little Thomases, not for other children. Please put it back," Mrs. Cotton said. Her mouth puckered out like she had just sucked on a lemon. Everybody could tell she wasn't playing around. Lena put the sandwich back on the plate. Lana looked at the floor. I felt terrible.

"That's not fair," I said to Mrs. Cotton. I was mad now, too. But it didn't seem to matter.

"Children must eat in their own homes," she said.

"We'll go," said Lana quietly.

"But where will you go?" I asked.

"Home," Lena said. I wondered if she had forgotten that they had lost their key. Lena lifted her head very high. I could tell she felt like crying. I thought about telling Mrs. Cotton what I knew. But I knew Lena and Lana probably wouldn't want me to, so I kept quiet.

Lena looked at Mrs. Cotton. "My aunt left some—"

"Peanut butter for us," Lana finished her sentence.

I knew they weren't telling the truth. But I didn't say anything. I just watched them go out the back door. Mrs. Cotton began to clean up the dishes.

"Eat your sandwich, Willimena," she said.

"No!" I said.

She looked at me and then she sighed. "Suit yourself," she said, and went back to cleaning up. But I wasn't hungry before, and I sure wasn't hungry now.

I went outside to look for Lena and Lana. I knew they were locked out of their house, but I hoped that maybe they had a secret way to get in. But even if they could get in, I knew they probably didn't have anything to eat. I thought again about the secret they had told me when they first moved to our street.

"If we tell you something, do you promise not to tell?" Lana had said.

"Sure," I said.

Lena scowled at Lana. "Aunt Wynn said not to tell our business," she said.

"I won't tell anybody," I said.

"You promise?" Lena said.

"I promise," I said. I wondered what it could be.

"Our mom is real sick," Lana said. "We're living with Aunt Wynn until she gets better."

"Aunt Wynn works nights," said Lena.

"And sometimes days," Lana said.

"Aunt Wynn doesn't have a lot of money. Sometimes we have to make breakfast last," Lena added.

"And last and last and last," Lana continued.

"Don't you get hungry?" I'd asked. They looked at the ground and then at each other and then away.

"Sometimes," Lana said.

I knew they must be hungry now. I wondered what I should do.

When I couldn't find Lena and Lana I started to look for Amber. Lydia told me that she had gone shopping with her mother, so I watched some TV with Tina and Lydia. Since I hadn't had any lunch, I got hungry after about an hour and went down to the kitchen to make myself a peanut-butter-and-jelly sandwich. But when I started to eat it, I started to think about Lena and Lana, so I didn't enjoy it.

The thought that they were probably still hungry stayed on my mind like a pebble does under your toe when it gets caught in your sneaker.

The Cookie Money

If you haven't guessed already, I'll tell you what happened to the cookie money. I spent it on Lana and Lena. After they told me how they never got lunch, I bought it for them. I didn't tell them where I got the money, I just spent it like it belonged to me.

I bought Lena and Lana lunch every day for two weeks. Each day we'd go to the pizzeria on the corner and buy a slice of pizza. Sometimes we'd buy two slices. Once or twice we bought a submarine sandwich. We always bought sodas. On the way home, we usually stopped at the bakery next to the pizzeria and bought some brownies. Lena and Lana would save theirs to eat at night. I'd eat mine before I got home so Tina wouldn't want any.

I was still worried about Lena and Lana the night after Mrs. Cotton made them go home. I couldn't go to sleep. I was wondering where they had gone, and why I hadn't seen them when I went outside. Maybe one of them had found the key or called their aunt. Or maybe they had just wandered around hungry with no place to go. Then I began to think about the cookie money. It was Monday night. If I didn't find a way to put it back, in six days everybody would know that I had spent it. I wondered what I was going to do.

I tried to think of an excuse to tell Mrs. Jones. Maybe I could tell her that somebody had stolen the money. But my parents would know that wasn't the truth. And what's worse, I'd know it, too. Maybe I could say that I lost the money, that I'd put it in a paper sack the way I'd put the candy on Halloween. I could say there was a hole in the bag and all the money had fallen out. Should I just tell Mrs. Jones the truth? I wondered.

But then I started to imagine about what people would say. Everybody would know what I had done, that I spent money that didn't belong to me. I would probably end up getting kicked out of Brownies. I'd never heard of anybody getting kicked out of Brownies. It was probably one of the worst things that could happen to a kid, like getting kicked out of nursery school. It was the kind of thing nobody would forget. I tossed and turned some more.

"Go to sleep, Willie. You're keeping me awake," Tina said. Her bed is on the other side of the room, but I guess she could hear me moving around.

"I can't."

"Count fish," Tina said.

In some families, people count sheep. In mine we count fish. One when the fish jumps out of the water. Two when he dives back in. Three when the next fish jumps out. Four when he dives back in. And on. And on. It's the most boring thing in the world. But it works. I'm usually asleep before the tenth fish jumps and dives.

It didn't work this time. The fish made me think about fried porgies. That's my favorite meal. Then I thought about Lena and Lana again. I wondered what they had had for dinner. They made me remember the cookie money and how $5.75 was all that was left. I started to worry again about what I would say when my mom asked me to get it on Monday. Then my pillow fell on the floor. When I reached down to get it, I knocked off the lamp near my bed.

"What in the world is wrong with you?" Tina yelled.

"I've got a lot of things on my mind," I said as I got back into bed.

"Like what?"

"Stuff."

"I'm sorry about the syrup," she said. Tina must have thought I was still mad at her, even though I'd almost forgotten about it.

"I'm sorry, too. About kicking you," I said.

"I'm sorry about the remote last night," she said.

"I'm sorry about the chocolate syrup," I said.

"I forgive you," Tina said.

"I forgive you, too," I said.

"Now go to sleep," Tina said.

But I couldn't. "You still awake, Tina?" I asked after a while.

"Yeah."

"Did you think that Mrs. Cotton was mean to Lena and Lana today?"

"Yeah! She's always being mean to somebody," Tina said.

"Did you know that Lena and Lana don't get enough to eat?"

Tina didn't say anything. I thought maybe she was asleep, but then she said, "Really?"

"Remember how last week when we all went to get a slice of pizza and Lena and Lana bought a whole pie then had it for lunch for the next few days?"

Tina was quiet for a moment. "That was weird," she said.

"You know how every day after me and you get lunch me and Lena and Lana go to the pizzeria, and how they always come back with cookies and soda?"

"Yeah. That's really cool!" Tina said.

"Remember how last week they came

back with that big turkey-and-cheese submarine, and they ate half and then Mrs. Washington gave them some aluminum foil, and they took it home with them when they left?"

"Yeah. Their aunt must be the bomb giving them all that money to spend on food," Tina said.

"They didn't get the money from their aunt," I said.

"Then where do they get it?"

"They got it from me," I said.

Tina sat up in bed. "From you, Willie! Where did you get it?"

"I gave them the cookie money," I said.

Tina gasped. Then she sucked her teeth loud. She sounded just like Mrs. Cotton, but I didn't tell her that. "Wow! You gave all that money, the whole twenty dollars, to Lena and Lana?"

"Yeah," I said.

"Why?"

"I told you. Because they were hungry," I said.

Tina didn't say anything for a very long while. There was no noise at all in our room. I thought she had gone to sleep. But then she sat up again.

"That's a drag, Willie."

"I know," I said.

It was quiet in our room for a few minutes more. Then Tina said in a sad voice, "I'm sorry I told Dad about the cookie money this morning. I just wanted to get you in trouble because you kicked me so hard. You know it really hurt. You've never kicked me like that before."

"Well, I was mad because you took all the syrup," I said.

"Well, I told you I was sorry for that," Tina said.

"Well, I said I was sorry, too," I said. "For kicking you. That hard, anyway."

"So what are you going to do when

Monday comes?" Tina asked.

"I don't know, Tina. I just don't know!" Then I did something that I hate to do more than anything in the world, especially in front of Tina, who always calls me a baby, which is the worst thing in the world to call somebody. I started to cry. Just like a baby. I tried to hide the sound in my pillow, but I couldn't. I was crying too loud. I cried for Lena and Lana and because their mother was sick. I cried because I hated how mean Mrs. Cotton had been to them. And I cried because I had spent the cookie money and let everybody down.

Then Tina did something that made me forgive her for all the mean stuff she'd ever done to me. She came and sat down on my bed. She put her arms around me and held me very tight.

"Don't worry, Willie. I'll come up with a plan," she said.

"What kind of a plan, Tina?"

"I don't know yet." I knew she was narrowing her eyes and looking around the room. That's what Tina does when she thinks hard. "It will have to be something where we can make money fast. By next Monday."

"But what, Tina? What?" I felt like crying again.

Even though it was dark, I knew Tina was looking in my direction.

"I don't know, but it will be something good. Have I ever let you down before?"

I could think of at least five times when she had, but I didn't say it. I knew she'd done the best she could.

"Don't worry, Willie. Now go to sleep," she said.

And I did.

The Greenes' Backyard

The next morning I asked Tina about her plan.

"I'm still thinking," Tina said. I asked her again while we were eating breakfast. "Give me some time!" she said.

"Have you had enough time?" I asked her when we went out to play.

"Don't be so impatient, Willie!" Tina tried to sound like my mom does when she says it to me. Usually it bothers me when she tries to sound like a grown-up, but I didn't care today. I was too worried.

"Have you had enough time yet?" I asked Tina at lunch. We were eating peanut-butter-and-jelly sandwiches. Tina likes chocolate-chip cookies crumbled up with peanut butter and jelly. She takes a chocolate-chip cookie, crumbles it up, and sprinkles it on her sandwich. She says it makes the sandwich taste like a candy bar. At least it's not as bad as the ketchup and tuna fish.

"Great ideas are like little birds, Willie. They take a long time to hatch," Tina said. She sounded like my grandma this time. She took a bite of her sandwich and peered at me with a serious look on her face. "You can't come up with a good plan overnight. Sometimes it takes a couple of days."

"I don't have a couple of days!" I wondered if Tina had forgotten that Monday was just a couple of days away.

"Don't worry, little sister," Tina said.

That's another thing I don't like, when she calls me "little sister." I decided to ignore it.

"When, Tina?"

"I can feel it forming in my mind, word by word," Tina said. She closed her eyes and touched the side of her head. Then she rubbed it, as if she could feel something moving around inside. "End of the day, Willie. End of the day," she said. "I'll tell you at the meeting when I tell everybody else."

"Meeting? Why can't you tell me now?" I wanted to know. But Tina just smiled mysteriously. My mom says Tina might be an actress when she grows up. She calls Tina a drama queen because she likes to be dramatic. She says I'm going to be either a scientist or a newspaper reporter like her because I'm curious about everything.

After lunch, Tina and I went back outside to play. Our house is on the end of the block. Next door to us live Amber and Lydia. Next to them live Betty and Booker. Their grandmother, Mrs. Smith, lives with them and their parents. She goes to Mrs. Cotton's church. Mrs. Smith is the reason my mother hired Mrs. Cotton. Except for that, Mrs. Smith is really great. She makes the best oatmeal-and-raisin cookies I've ever had in my life. I could eat them for every meal every day of the week.

Betty is eight, a year older than me. Booker is four, three years younger. He does anything anybody tells him to do. He even lets me tell him what to do. But he's a nice little kid and that's why we let him hang out with us. Betty is bossy. Amber and I call her a Tina-in-training.

The Greenes live next to Betty and Booker. There are so many people in the Greene family, it's hard to count them all. Once I thought that there were only five. But then two cousins moved in from

Detroit. Now there are seven. They all have round faces and big teeth, even the cousins, and they all have the same laugh. It starts like a giggle, gets real loud, and then ends up in a giggle again. They also all have names that begin with G.

The oldest Greene is Gregory. He's eleven, two years older than Tina, which makes him the oldest kid on the block. Then comes George, who is nine, the same age as Tina. But Tina is a month older. After George comes Grace, who is six. Then comes Gerry. I don't know how old he is, because he doesn't say much. The baby, Ginger, is about two years old. Then come the cousins, Gandy and Golden. They always come at the end of school and stay all summer. Gandy is six and Golden is eight.

Next to the Greenes lives Mrs. Pyle. Mrs. Pyle lives by herself. She always complains when the Greenes' soccer balls roll into her yard. She also complains about the noise when we all play in the Greenes' backyard, which is almost every day. She doesn't like animals much either. Each of the Greene children has a pet, and Mrs. Pyle complains about the pets.

Pauline lives next to Mrs. Pyle. Besides Amber, Pauline is my best friend on the street. We're born on the very same day in the very same month. Pauline loves to draw. She can draw anything you ask her to. She also has a great baby-sitter named Candy. Candy is a teenager. She always styles our hair in new styles and lets us put on makeup. She also paints our finger- and toenails. Candy has the prettiest nail polishes I've ever seen. My favorite is egg-plant, which is dark purple and looks great. My mom doesn't like it, though. She always makes me take it off.

Pauline is the only kid on the block who has ever been inside Mrs. Pyle's house. She says that Mrs. Pyle makes really good fudge, and that she has a cute little canary named Tweetie. She's the only kid who has ever seen him.

Besides Candy, the other great thing Pauline has are earrings. Her father travels to different countries, and he always brings back earrings. She has about a hundred pairs of earrings, even though she's only seven years old.

Lena and Lana live with their aunt Wynn in the last house. Now that they've moved in, every house on our side of the street is filled with kids, except for Mrs. Pyle's. In the summer, everybody on the street plays together until it gets dark. Sometimes we play girls only, and the boys play by themselves. Sometimes we all play together. The only person who plays with both girls and boys is Booker. He'll play with anybody.

Almost every other day, somebody on

our street will call a block meeting. Then we will all meet in the Greenes' backyard, because it's the biggest. Tina called a meeting today, and the word spread quickly.

"Greenes' yard after dinner," everybody said. But it probably wasn't necessary. We all usually end up in the Greenes' backyard after dinner anyway.

The Greenes' house is big and about a hundred years old. It used to be a school, and the backyard used to be the playground. The backyard is very long and narrow. The grass is worn down, but the dirt is soft. It feels good under your feet when you take off your shoes. One side of the yard belongs to Mrs. Greene. She likes to plant vegetables and flowers. My mom says she has a green thumb because everything she plants takes root. When I was little, I used to think her thumb was the color of broccoli, which is kind of sickening when you think about it. But now I know it just means she's a good gardener. Her thumb is brown, the same color as mine.

There is always something good to eat growing in Mrs. Greene's garden. She grows tomatoes, squash, and even corn. Flowers always seem to be in bloom in her garden, too. I love the irises, which look like they're all dressed up with no place to go. I like the impatiens, which come in all diferent shades of pink and red. My favorites are the black-eyed Susans that look like fancy daisies with a serious summer tan. Mrs. Greene doesn't like us to get too close to her garden, but sometimes she'll let us pick some of the flowers. She says that the other side of the yard is for kids, so that's where we always go. That's Mr. Greene's side.

Mr. Greene likes to fix things. If anybody on the block brings him something, he can fix it. His side of the yard is filled with broken stuff—bicycles and tricycles, a table or two. There's even a rocking chair that only rocks if somebody pushes it. He also has a mattress lying on the side of the house. Sometimes Gregory turns it over, and we all jump on it.

At the end of the Greenes' long backyard is the merry-go-round. It's the best thing on the block. The merry-go-round is as old as the house, but it still works. It used to be rusty, but Mr. Greene painted it bright blue. It's not fancy like a carousel in a park with horses and carriages and everything. It's shaped like a giant blueberry pie. It's fastened deep into the ground in the middle, and one side tilts until it twirls. You hold on to one of the handles attached to the sides. Then you run as fast as you can. When it's whirling fast, you jump on. It's the greatest feeling in the world. You close your eyes and you can hear the wind swish past your ears and cool your face. When you open them, everything swirls all around in a blur. You get so dizzy you can't walk for a minute or two. All you can do is fall on the ground and laugh.

But today, when it was time for the block meeting, nobody rode on the merry-go-round. Nobody smelled Mrs. Greene's flowers or bounced on the mattress that lay on the side of the house. Everybody just sat on the ground and listened to what Tina had to say.

I wished she had told me what she was going to say before the meeting, but I had to wait like everybody else. I thought about what my mom said about Tina being a drama queen. When the meeting was ready to start, Tina pulled over one of the old mattresses and stood on top of it. Everybody got quiet. Tina cleared her throat.

"A kid I know lost some money that didn't belong to her. If she doesn't get it back by Monday she could go to jail," Tina said.

"That's dumb! They don't put kids in jail!" George said.

"Who lost the money?" asked Gregory.

"Someone everybody knows," said Tina. I stared at the ground. Even though Tina hadn't mentioned my name, I was sure everybody knew it was me.

"How did she lose it?" asked Gregory.

"None of your business," Tina said in the bossy voice that said she meant business. For once, I was glad to hear it. "But I have a plan to make the money back. I need everybody's help."

Nobody said anything. My heart skipped a beat.

"Sure, we'll help," Gregory said after a minute. "What's your plan?"

Tina smiled. "Lemonade! Willie and I are going to have a lemonade sale to help the person who lost it get back her money.

62

We want everybody to say that they will buy some."

Everybody was quiet. Then they began to laugh.

"That's the dumbest idea I ever heard," said George Greene.

"Tina! Is that the big plan you've been thinking of all day? What kind of plan is that?" I yelled out. I couldn't believe what Tina had just said.

"Nobody sells lemonade anymore!" said Gandy.

"That doesn't even work on TV!" said Gerald.

"Plus, who's going to buy lemonade from kids on the street when they can get it at home?" asked George.

"Maybe you should come up with another idea," said Pauline in a soft voice. I had never heard Pauline yell or say anything mean to anybody.

"It will work," Tina said with a smile. I

knew the smile. It was the smile she always got when she held all the aces in war or was about to get the last spoon of peanut butter. It was the smile that meant she was determined to win.

"Maybe it will," said Amber. She knew that smile, too.

"We said we'd help, so we will," said Gregory quietly. "Tina and . . . her friend . . . need help. It's the spirit of the block to help out people who live here."

At that moment, I thought Gregory was the smartest, kindest kid I'd ever known in my life. I felt like giving him a hug, but I knew he'd be embarrassed.

"We might help by buying it if it doesn't cost too much, but we're not going to help make it," said George. Everybody nodded in agreement. But I had my doubts.

"Are you sure it's going to work, Tina?"

I asked her that night before we went to sleep.

"Don't worry, Willie," Tina said. "Don't I always keep my word?"

Sometimes it's best to keep your thoughts to yourself.

The Lemonade Sale

The next morning started out like any other. My mom called me and Tina down for breakfast. We drank our juice and ate our cereal. My mom left for work. My dad left for school. Mrs. Cotton called us little Thomases. Everything was the same. Except that it was Wednesday. There were five more days until the cookie money was due. I usually believe Tina when she smiles her winner's smile. But this time I had my doubts, even though she acted as if she knew what she was doing.

Before we went outside, Tina wrote down the things we needed to have to make the lemonade sale a success. Tina loves to write cursive. She holds the pencil just so. She sits straight at the table. She puts her tongue on her top lip. Every letter, every curve, every dot, every crossed "t" is perfect. She writes cursive better than anybody I know.

When she wrote, she used her fanciest handwriting and the colored pencils my grandma gave her. She wrote each word in a different color. *Lemons* was in yellow. *Cups* was in blue and *sugar* in orange, because white wouldn't show up on paper. Then she read the list aloud.

"You need something to make the lemonade in," I suggested.

"Like a pan or a pot or something," she said, agreeing.

Then she wrote *big pot* in purple.

"Done! Now we have to buy all the ingredients."

"What do we have to buy?"

"Sugar and lemons, of course," she said.

"How are we going to buy them? We don't have any money?" Tina studied me for a moment and then smiled. It was the smile she wore when she knew something I didn't. It was the one she had when she learned to write cursive and rode her bike without training wheels for the first time. It always reminded me that she was my big sister and knew how to do things I didn't.

"It takes money to make money," Tina said. "You'll have to spend some of the money you have left."

She was talking about the five dollars and seventy-five cents that was left from the cookie money.

"No!" I said.

"How else are we going to buy the lemons and sugar?" she asked.

"We have instant lemonade leftover from last summer," I said, even though I knew that wouldn't work. "Or we can take the sugar from the sugar bowl and use the lemon juice in the refrigerator."

"Nobody will buy lemonade made from bottled lemon juice. We have to make it from scratch. You can't use a mix. We have to use real lemons and lots of sugar," Tina said.

"Then we can borrow the lemons from Amber's mother," I said. Amber's mother likes to make pies, cookies, and cakes. She always has stuff like lemons. "We can borrow the sugar, too."

"Get the money, Willie," Tina said impatiently.

I went into the purple tin in the drawer in our bedroom. I got out the last of the money, all $5.75. We asked Mrs. Cotton if we could go to the corner. She said that we could as long as we didn't cross the main street.

"Somebody making lemonade?" said Mr. Curtis, the owner of Curtis's Fine Groceries, the store at the corner. "Looks like somebody's going on a picnic!"

"We're going to sell it," I said.

"Great idea!" Mr. Curtis said. He wiped his forehead. "It's a great day for a lemonade sale!"

Tina grinned. I did, too. Maybe Tina's plan would work after all.

We bought eight lemons, which came to $2.00. We bought five pounds of sugar for $2.00 and three dozen small paper cups for $1.75.

The cookie money was completely gone now. I tried not to think about it.

When we came back from the store, we went to Amber and Lydia's house to drop off everything we'd bought. They said we could make it at their house instead of at home. We knew Mrs. Cotton would be afraid we'd make a mess. Mrs.

Washington, Amber and Lydia's mother, gave us permission to use her kitchen and one of her big pots if we promised to clean up. During the school year, Mrs. Washington teaches third grade. She loves to give kids projects.

Tina drew up what she and Lydia called a plan of action. We decided that the sale would be at 1:30 P.M., after everybody came back from lunch. We would set up the stand on the street in front of Lena and Lana's house, because their house was on the corner nearest to the main street. We could get customers coming from every direction. We decided to sell the lemonade for seventy-five cents a cup. We knew it was a lot of money, but Tina said we'd call it the "Best Lemonade in the World." We hoped that people would believe it.

When Tina and Lydia had finished the plan of action, they read off everyone's chores. She and Lydia decided that they would make the lemonade. Amber and I would make the signs and hang them all around the street.

"Why can't we make lemonade, too?" Amber asked.

"Because you can't," said Lydia.

"Can we help make it?" I asked Lydia. Making the signs for a lemonade sale certainly wasn't as much fun as making the lemonade.

"No," Tina said.

"Just do what we say," added Lydia.

"You can't tell Willie what to do," Amber said to Lydia.

"Girls!" Mrs. Washington warned from the next room. She sounded just like my mother.

"It was my idea," said Tina to me. "So I get to do the fun thing."

"But I'm the one who needs the money," I said, but nobody seemed to hear me. "You have to let me help!"

Tina turned and glared at me. "Willie, do you even know how to make lemonade?" she asked. Suddenly Tina was acting just like my bossy older sister again. The nice Tina who had given me the hug last night had disappeared.

"No. And you don't, either!" I said. We sounded like the Sisters Umoja again. I could almost hear my father's voice.

"Yes, I do. I helped my teacher make it in school for our bake sale. I know *exactly* what to do," Tina said. "Plus, you and Amber are *younger* than me and Lydia. There's a lot of responsibility that goes into making lemonade for a lemonade sale. You and Amber are just *too young* to take on all that responsibility. But after you have made the signs, you and Amber can watch," Tina said. "And then someday you'll be old enough to make lemonade, too!"

"Oh, whoop-de-do! Aren't we lucky!" said

Amber. Tina could see that I was getting mad.

"I'll tell you what. You two can wash the lemons," Tina said. "But don't use soap. Just water."

"I know not to use soap on lemons!" I said angrily. "You think you know everything. Don't be such a brat, Tina."

"You're a brat!" Tina said back.

"I hope your lemonade stinks!" I said.

"Ungrateful thing!" Tina said. I was quiet then. I knew that we shouldn't fight anymore in front of Mrs. Washington. I was also afraid that maybe I was being ungrateful. So Amber and I got some typing paper from Mrs. Washington and carefully printed the signs. They all said the same thing:

Best Lemonade in the World
75¢ a Cup

Then we got ready to make the lemonade. First, we all washed our hands carefully. Amber and I washed the lemons. Lydia and Tina got a cutting board, and Mrs. Washington helped them cut the lemons in half. Then they squeezed the lemons into a bowl and poured it into the pot. Lydia added water. Tina poured in sugar. Then she tasted it. She added some more sugar. Then she tasted it again, and poured in some more. A lot more. Mrs. Washington helped them put the pot into the refrigerator so that it would get cold.

Just as we were getting ready to hang the signs, Lena and Lana came walking down the street. I was really glad to see them.

"Where have you two been?" I asked.

They glanced at each other and didn't say anything for a moment. "We went to see my mom," Lana finally said in a soft voice.

"Is she better?" I asked as quietly as I could.

"A little bit," said Lena. "I think she'll be okay soon."

I could tell by the way she said it that they were both worried about their mom. I got mad all over again at Mrs. Cotton for being so mean to them.

"What're you doing?" Lena asked.

"Hanging signs."

"Why are you having a lemonade sale?" Lana asked.

"To make some money," Amber said. I was happy she didn't say why we had to make money. I didn't want Lena and Lana to guess what had happened.

"Can we help you hang some, too?" Lana asked.

I gave her four of the signs, and we all began to put them up. We put one on the windshield of the Greenes' car, and another on our mailbox. Mr. Curtis let us hang two in his store window. I had my doubts about customers coming all the way from his store to buy a cup of lemonade, even if it was the "Best Lemonade in the World," but Tina said it was good business. We put one on every tree that we saw. Soon, almost everywhere you looked on our street there was a sign for lemonade.

After lunch, we got a table from the Greenes' backyard and set it up in front of Lena and Lana's house. Mrs. Washington brought the lemonade out with a big cup for Tina to serve it with. We were ready to go.

Gregory Greene was the first customer.

"Here's my money," he said. I took his seventy-five cents and put it into the purple tin box. Soon there was a line of kids from our street and one or two new kids from another. Then the mailman joined the line. A man who was delivering packages got in line, and Candy, Pauline's baby-sitter got in line, too. Even Mrs. Cotton came out and got in line. Maybe Mr.

Curtis was right, that people would buy lemonade because it was a hot day.

"I'll take two," said Mrs. Washington. She gave us a dollar and fifty cents.

"Give us two," Lena and Lana said. I wondered where they had gotten the money, but I didn't ask. I was too happy to get it.

"I'll take three. One for me and two for my parents when they get home from work," said Pauline.

"Great!" I said, as I poured her three cups.

"I'll take two, too. Just to help out," said Candy.

In ten minutes, we had made ten dollars. Things were looking up. Then George Greene held out his seventy-five cents.

"One," he said, and I gave him a cup. He dropped his seventy-five cents into the can. He took a sip. Then he scowled. Then he took another sip. Then he spit it out.

"Yuck!" he said. "This junk stinks! It's terrible!" He bent over and grabbed his stomach as if he was going to throw up.

I looked around at the other customers. Everyone was talking quietly. Some people had poured their lemonade out on the ground. Some had poured it on bushes. Most people had poured it in the gutter.

Nobody was drinking it. The kids who had been in line behind George stepped out of line.

"False advertising! False advertising!" George Greene yelled. "This isn't the best lemonade in the world. This is the *worst* lemonade in the world!"

Several kids started to laugh. I looked at Amber. She wouldn't look me in the eye. Lena and Lana started to giggle.

I poured a cup for myself.

George was right. It tasted horrible. It tasted just like sugar and water. I couldn't taste any lemons at all.

"Tina! Taste the lemonade," I whispered.

Tina stopped pouring a cup and gulped it down quickly.

"Tastes all right to me," she said.

"No, it doesn't," I whispered again.

"It tastes good, Willie," she drank another cup.

Suddenly I understood the miserable truth. How would someone who liked ketchup on tuna fish know how good lemonade would taste?

"I want my money back!" yelled George Greene.

"Sorry!" said Tina. "You paid for it. There's nothing wrong with the lemonade."

"Give me my seventy-five cents back!" yelled George.

"No!" Tina yelled back. Tina set her mouth into the line that meant she wasn't going to budge. I knew that mouth well.

"Give it back!" said George again.

George set his mouth into a line, too. He was as determined as Tina.

"No," Tina said.

I don't like to think about what happened next. George tried to get his money out of my tin box. Tina tried to stop him. George shoved Tina out of the way. Tina shoved him back. George fell into the table and knocked over the lemonade stand. The lemonade pot tipped over. Lemonade was everywhere! It fell on George and Tina. It dripped down the side of the Greenes' old table and onto the sidewalk. It flowed in front of Lena and Lana's house and down the street toward Pauline's like a river.

"You're disgusting, George Greene!" Tina screamed. "Look what you made me do!"

Ginger Greene got on her knees and started to play in it. She tasted it and smiled at Tina. "Good!" she said as she licked her fingers.

"No, no, Ginger," Grace said and picked

up her little sister. Ginger started to cry, and Mrs. Greene came running outside to see what had happened.

"What a mess! George, did you have something to do with this?" she asked.

George dropped his head. Mrs. Greene made George go inside, and his brothers and sisters followed behind him. The lemonade turned into sticky puddles all over the sidewalk and street. It was the worst mess I'd ever seen.

Although I hadn't done anything wrong, I still felt bad. George shouldn't have shoved Tina, but he was right. The lemonade was the worst in the world. Amber, Lydia, Lena, and Lana helped us gather up everything and take it back inside, and then everybody went back home.

"I guess you were right about the lemonade. It really did stink," Tina said before we went to sleep that night. I couldn't believe what I was hearing. Tina never admitted she was wrong about something, especially not to me. "I'm sorry my plan didn't work."

"That's okay, Tina. You did your best," I said.

Soon she was asleep. I could hear her snoring. I lay awake for a while. For the first time that I could remember, Tina had actually admitted I was right. I was glad about that. But except for the ten dollars I'd made today, I still didn't have the cookie money. It was up to me now to come up with my own plan.

Doofus Doolittle

My granddad says that when you need to find an answer to a problem you should sleep on it. I didn't know what he meant at first, and then my mom explained. If you ask yourself a question before you go to sleep, then your mind will work on it while you're asleep. You'll have the answer when you wake up the next morning. The night after the nasty lemonade sale I decided to take my granddad's advice. Before I went to sleep, I wrote a question on a sheet of paper. The question was:

How should I earn back the cookie money?

I folded up the paper, put it under my pillow, and slept on it like my granddad said to do. That night I dreamed about Doofus Doolittle.

Doofus Doolittle is not an ordinary cat. His fur is black and shiny. He has big golden eyes that sometimes look half-closed. He is very curious and always sticks his nose where it's not supposed to be. If I were a cat or he were a girl, we'd be best friends. In my dream, his furry little face was next to mine. He touched my nose with his cold little nose, just the way he does when he wakes me up sometimes. It was as if he were trying to tell me a secret.

When my mom called me the next morning for breakfast, I jumped out of bed fast. We were having pancakes again. Twice in one week was great. I didn't want to take any chances that Tina might get the last drop of orange juice or pat of butter. Then Doofus Doolittle came into my room and rubbed up against my leg. It was like he was reminding me of something. My dream came back.

I picked him up and gave him a hug. I love to feel his warm little face against my own. I even gave him a kiss on the chin like I do when nobody's looking. He tilted his head to the side and meowed. Sometimes, I think Doofus is the cutest cat I've ever seen. He's even cuter than the cats in magazines or the ones you see on TV. And then the answer to my problem came to me.

Every kid on our street thought that his or her pet was the cutest in the world. Lydia and Amber thought Snowflake, their white Persian cat, was the cutest. Booker and Betty have hamsters. They thought they were the cutest. The Greenes have two dogs, goldfish, and two birds. They all thought their pets were the best. The answer to my cookie-money problem was all the cute, smart animals on the block. In other words, a pet show to decide whose pet was *really* the best.

I could call it the Oak Street Pet Show. I would charge each kid on the block a fee to enter his or her pet in the show. I would also charge kids who didn't have pets an admission fee. I would make *mad* money. Hand over fist. More maybe even than I needed.

I pulled on my jeans and my sneakers. Then I ran downstairs as fast as I could. I could hardly wait to tell Tina about my plan. This was the best idea I had ever had.

"Morning . . . Willie," Tina said when I sat down. Both my mom and dad were sitting down at the table. I figured that was why she didn't call me the usual name. My dad smiled at her approvingly.

"I'm happy you remembered, Tina," he said.

"We really are the Umoja sisters this morning, aren't we girls?" my mother said as she got ready to go to work. Me and Tina both nodded that we were. When my dad went to get his backpack, I told Tina about my idea. She agreed that it was a winner.

"First make a list, Willie," Tina said. "The first thing you have to do whenever you get an idea is make a list."

I finished breakfast and then went outside to look for Amber. Lena and Lana were playing on her front porch, even thought it was still early. When I told them my idea, they agreed that it was a good one.

"What do you have to—" began Lena.

"Do first?" asked Lana. I told them what Tina had said. I borrowed a piece of paper from Mrs. Washington's notepad and sat down on the porch beside them.

"What's going to be on the list?" asked Amber. The four of us sat there for a while trying to figure out what to write. I thought of asking Tina, but I didn't want her to know that I couldn't figure it out for myself. Then I thought about what my mom said that reporters ask themselves when they report a story. She said they always ask themselves the five Ws. I thought hard, trying to figure out what they were. Then I remembered: Who, What, Where, When, and Why.

So I wrote down the first W—Who. I wrote down my name. Willie Thomas. Then I wrote down the Oak Street Association. I liked the way it sounded— official. What—a pet show. When—tomorrow afternoon. Where—the Greenes' yard. I paused for a minute. I'd have to ask the Greenes if it was okay, but I knew they'd say that it was. Why—to find the cutest, smartest pet on Oak Street.

I read my list over. Then I wrote down the things to do: 1. Ask Gregory Greene's permission for his backyard. 2. Make and hang signs. 3. Find a judge. 4. Make a plaque for first prize. 5. Get Doofus ready.

The first two steps were easy. I asked Amber, Lena, and Lana to help me collect the signs we'd used for the lemonade sale. We printed new signs about the pet show on the back of the old signs.

Is your pet cute?
Is your pet talented?
Enter your pet in the
Oak Street Pet Show.
75¢ Pet Admission
50¢ Without Pet

We hung the new signs in the same places we'd hung the signs for the lemonade.

I hoped that the bad luck we'd had with the lemonade sale wouldn't rub off on the pet show. I asked Candy, Pauline's baby-sitter, if she would be the judge. She is always fair and never takes sides. Then I made a first prize. I took a square piece of wood and covered it with tin foil. I pasted gold stamps all around it. Then I took a big blue ribbon and attached it to the end. I asked Tina to write in cursive "Cutest, Smartest Pet on Oak Street" on a piece of white paper and glued it in the middle.

The first four things were crossed off my list. The next thing was Doofus Doolittle. He has a mind of his own. He never does what anybody says. If you give him dried cat food, he cries until you give him canned food. If you give him canned food, he cries until you give him dried. When you put him outside, he wants to come in. If you bring him in, he wants to go back out. He hates to go to the vet, and when we take him, my dad has to spell out the word *vet* or Doofus will disappear and then come back home late at night, after the vet is closed. The only thing that Doofus Doolittle hates more than the vet is taking a bath. I knew that giving him a bath for the pet show was out of the question. So I decided I would just brush his hair and tie a red ribbon around his neck.

Besides being cute, especially when he has on a red ribbon, Doofus Doolittle also does tricks. His best one is opening a door. He hooks his paw underneath it and pulls hard. If it's not closed too tight, the door always comes open. He's also a whiz when it comes to finding his toy mouse. My mom bought Doofus Doolittle a little gray-and-brown mouse. It slides across the floor when you push it. Doofus Doolittle can always find the mouse no matter where it slides. When you toss it down, he'll chase it and bring it back to you in one minute flat.

Finally everything was ready. Everybody on the street was excited. Everybody had brushed, washed, or rehearsed their pet. Everybody was sure their pet would win. That night I dreamed about Doofus Doolittle in his red ribbon. In my dream, I'd taught him how to play "Chopsticks" on the piano. He could bang out the melody with his little paws as well as anyone I've ever heard. I woke up the next morning thinking about how he really was the best pet in the world. Even if he couldn't play a note.

The Pet Show

I was so excited about the pet show I almost forgot what day it was. But then I remembered. It was Friday. I only had three more days to earn back the cookie money. I had a lot riding on the pet show. But it was going to be a success. I knew it. After breakfast I went outside to get things ready. I found a tin can to put the money in and placed it on the old table in the Greenes' backyard. The table only had three legs, so Gregory helped me balance it with a stack of magazines. Then I sat down behind the table. Because I was running the contest, Tina entered Doofus Doolittle. Her seventy-five cents were the first coins to drop into the tin can. Lana and Lena stood beside Tina.

"I wish we—" started Lena.

"Could have a pet, but Aunt Wynn—" added Lana.

"Doesn't like animals—"

"Not even birds!" Lana said. "So we'll cheer for Doolittle—"

"Doofus," finished Lena.

"Doofus Doolittle," Tina corrected.

"Doofus Doolittle!" Lena and Lana said together.

Lena took Doofus Doolittle from Tina and hugged him. He brushed her nose with his the same way he does mine.

Amber and Lydia were next in line. I knew they thought Snowflake, their pet cat, was going to win. I had to admit that

Snowflake was a pretty cat. Lydia had given her a bath and brushed her fur until it was fluffy and beautiful. Amber had tied a lacy pink ribbon around Snowflake's neck. She looked like the cats who advertise fancy cat food on TV. Lana petted the top of Snowflake's head. Snowflake looked at her and purred. I hoped Lana didn't decide to cheer for Snowflake instead of Doofus Doolittle.

But even if she did, I didn't think that Snowflake could beat Doofus Doolittle. The prize was for more than just being pretty. It was for personality and talent, too. Snowflake is beautiful, but Doofus Doolittle has a good personality. That was very important.

"Good luck!" I said to Amber. I wished I had thought of making two first-prize awards. But it was too late. Only one pet could get the award. I knew that Amber and Lydia would be disappointed if it wasn't Snowflake. But Tina and I would be disappointed if Doofus Doolittle didn't win.

Betty and Booker were the next kids in line. Betty was carrying her hamsters, Boo and Koo, in their cage. Booker was walking beside her.

"Aren't they cute?" said Betty with a grin.

"I hope Boo and Koo win!" added Booker. I smiled even though I really didn't think they had much of a chance. Hamsters are cute, but they don't do a lot of tricks. The only thing they can do is run around on their little wheel and drink water from their bottle. That didn't take much talent.

But I knew Betty and Booker would be so disappointed if their pets didn't win the contest. Why hadn't I thought about that? Why hadn't I made enough prizes for everybody?

The Greenes were the next kids in

line—the next five kids in line. I had promised Gregory that they could enter one of
their pets for free because the pet show
was going to be in their backyard, so I
didn't charge him for Casey, his dog. Casey
looks like three dogs rolled into one. He is
long and low to the ground like a dachs-
hund. He has a face like a cocker spaniel.
He sounds like a German shepherd when
he barks. He's the strangest-looking dog
I've ever seen. But he can run very fast,
even though his legs are short. Gregory
says he can run as fast as a greyhound.
Maybe he's four dogs mixed up into one.

George was next in line. He was enter-
ing Rusty, Mrs. Greene's dog before she got
married. Rusty is an Irish setter. He has
reddish fur that looks gold in the sunlight.
He's very old. Mrs. Greene says he's about
fifteen years old, which is nearly one hundred years old for people. Sometimes he
has a hard time walking. He doesn't get

outside very much. Mostly he likes to lie in the sun and sleep. I wished I'd thought of making a prize for oldest dog.

"How much money is the prize?" George asked as he dropped his seventy-five cents into the can.

"It's not money, it's a plaque," I said.

He looked doubtful. But George always looks doubtful. "That's not fair! Nobody wants a dumb plaque."

"Money isn't everything!" I said.

"So what kind of plaque is it?" he asked.

"You'll see if you win," I said.

I was starting to get a little worried. When I'd made the prize, I hadn't thought too much about it. What if the winner was disappointed? What if he or she wanted his or her money back? What if people didn't agree with Candy? Maybe the Oak Street Pet Show wasn't such a terrific idea after all.

Grace Greene entered her lovebirds,

Mitch and Match, who were sitting in their cage. I felt kind of bad when I took her seventy-five cents. She was sure her birds would win, but I didn't think they would. They were cute, but all I had ever see them do was sit in the cage Mr. Greene had found at the dump. The only thing they could do was coo. I didn't even think they could fly. But Grace really loved them. She thought they were the most beautiful, talented pets on the block. Gandy and Goldy, the Greenes' cousins from Detroit, were next in line. They entered their two goldfish, who they'd named after themselves—Gandy and Goldy. I was afraid they had about as much chance of winning the prize as Mitch and Match did. Why had I only made one first prize? I asked myself again.

Pauline, who is allergic to fur, was next in line. She was holding a bird in a cage, too. I knew it must be Tweetie, Mrs. Pyle's bird. Tweetie was a canary. He was bright yellow just like the bird in the cartoon. He had a sharp little beak that he was using to open a sunflower seed. His cage had a big red bow on top.

"Tweetie is visiting me. Mrs. Pyle is letting me take care of him while she is on vacation," Pauline said. She put the cage on the table because it was heavy. "She'll be so surprised when Tweetie wins the prize. I'll give it to her when she gets back. She'll probably put it on the wall right behind his cage."

"Good luck!" I said cheerfully, even though I didn't feel very cheerful. Everybody, even my next-to-best friend, was going to be disappointed.

Five or six kids who had heard about the pet show from other streets brought their pets, too. One girl brought a tiny kitten in a little straw basket that everybody wanted to pet. A boy named Leon brought a green snake that Booker and Betty were afraid of. Another kid brought a plastic bowl with colorful fish.

Everybody was smiling and happy. Everybody was sure that his or her pet would win. Even Tina was smiling. I was the only person in the whole backyard who wasn't smiling. I wished that I had thought of another idea or at least had made up enough prizes so that each kid would get one. I counted the money in the tin cup. There was about ten dollars now, but even that didn't make me feel better.

Everybody stood in a line. Everybody was nervous. I glanced at Tina. Doofus Doolittle was squirming and trying to get out of her arms. He doesn't like to be held. Lena patted his head to calm him down.

I cleared my throat. "Ladies and gentlemen. Welcome to the annual Oak Street Pet Show," I said in a loud voice. I'd said "annual" because it made it sound official.

But I wasn't sure there would be another one. Too many kids would be disappointed.

"Ladies and gentlemen! There aren't any grown-ups here," said George. A couple of kids giggled.

I started again. "Welcome to the Oak Street Pet Show. I'd like to introduce our judge, Candy Keene."

"Don't you mean Candy Cane?" George said. The same kids who had giggled before giggled again.

Candy threw him a mean look. It was the first time I'd ever seen Candy give any-body a mean look. George stopped giggling. Candy stood up straight. She's a teenager, but she really looks like a grown-up. Everybody knew she would be fair.

Since Booker and Betty were first in line, Candy judged their pets first.

"Nice pets." She said it fast as if she didn't really believe it.

Betty could tell. She looked hurt. "Don't

you like hamsters?" she asked.

Candy wrinkled up her nose. "They look too much like mice," she said. Candy looks like a grown-up, but sometimes she forgets to act like one. A real grown-up would never have said that. She wouldn't want to hurt Betty and Booker's feelings.

"He has talent, too. Do you want to see Boo's trick?" Betty asked.

"Okay," Candy sounded uncertain.

Betty opened the cage and took out the hamster. She held him next to her chest and pet him. "His trick is when he eats. His cheeks grow real big," she said. She puffed out her own cheeks until they were twice as big as they usually are. "Give me the carrot, Booker," she said. Booker gave her a carrot. She put it near Boo's mouth. Boo started to nibble it. He nibbled and nibbled until his cheeks were filled with food.

"That's not a trick, all hamsters and

guinea pigs do that," George said. He had come to the front of the line to see what was going on.

Betty ignored him. "Hold Boo for a minute, Candy. Then you'll see how cute he is," she said.

"No! He looks too much like a mouse," Candy said. I could tell by the look on Candy's face that she didn't want to hold Boo.

"But Boo is a *hamster*!" Betty said. She handed Boo to Candy just as Candy threw up her hands. Boo grabbed Candy's blouse with his tiny claws. Candy screamed. Boo slid down the front of Candy's blouse to the ground. Betty screamed. Boo scampered away. He ran as fast as his little legs could carry him.

That was when my dream about the Oak Street Pet Show turned into a nightmare.

Disaster!

Doofus Doolittle must have thought that Boo was a mouse, too. Maybe he thought he was his brown-and-gray toy. The moment he saw Boo run across the yard, Doofus Doolittle jumped out of Tina's arms. He sprang to the ground. He took off after Boo.

"Stop, Doofus Doolittle!" Tina screamed. But it was too late. Doofus Doolittle was on Boo's trail. His tail was switching to and fro as he ran after Boo as fast as he could.

"Oh, no! Your cat is going to get my hamster! Run, Boo, run!" Betty screamed. Suddenly Gregory's dog, Casey, broke away from him. He barked twice. Then he aimed his snout in the air. Then he bared his teeth. He turned in Doofus Doolittle's direction and off he went.

"Run, Doofus Doolittle! Run!" I screamed.

"Look out, Boo!" Betty yelled. "Don't let him catch you."

Boo ran in a circle. Doofus Doolittle ran behind him. Casey ran after Doofus Doolittle. Then Boo ran under the merry-go-round. Doofus Doolittle ran after him. Casey stood waiting for them to come out. Boo ran out and headed under the table. Doofus Doolittle chased after him. Casey followed Doofus Doolittle. Betty dove under the table to rescue Boo. I ducked under the table to rescue Doofus Doolittle. The table tipped over. Tweetie's cage fell on the ground.

Tweet! Tweet! Tweetie screeched.

"Oh, no! Oh, no!" screamed Pauline. She ran to pick up the cage just as Snowflake leaped out of Amber's arms. Snowflake landed in a mud puddle near the table. Then she hopped on top of Tweetie's cage and began to rattle it with her paws. I'd never seen Snowflake do anything except lie around. I couldn't believe she could jump so far so fast.

"Snowflake!" Amber screamed as she tried to pry her pet's claws off the cage. Suddenly Rusty rolled out of his spot in the sun. He started to howl as he strolled toward Snowflake. Snowflake jumped back into the mud and then headed up a tree. Everybody's pet was suddenly barking, howling, meowing, squeaking, or squawking. Betty and Booker began to wail.

Mrs. Greene came running out of the house waving her hands in the air. "What in the world is going on out here?" she yelled.

Doofus Doolittle ran into Mrs. Greene's garden. Casey chased him and trampled the irises. Snowflake screeched and tried to claw her way up the tree. Rusty stood underneath it, howling and growling. Tweetie was flying around his cage trying to get out. Mitch and Match were squawking in theirs.

Mrs. Greene looked around her backyard. It was a mess. The magazines that Gregory had placed under the table were spread out on the ground. Torn paper was everywhere.

"I think it's time for everybody to go home!" said Mrs. Greene. She grabbed Rusty by his collar and pulled him from under the tree. "I will be back out here in ten minutes. I want my children in this house and all other children and animals out of my backyard!" she said. She slammed the door behind her. Mrs. Greene had never yelled at anyone before. I wondered if we'd ever be able to play in her backyard again.

"What a dumb idea this pet show was!" Gregory said.

"Yeah!" said the kid who had the snake.

"Look what happened to Snowflake!" Amber said as she pulled her pet out of the tree. "This is bad news. Real bad news!" Snowflake's pink ribbon was nowhere to be seen, and she was covered with mud.

"We'll have to take her to the vet to get her groomed!" Lydia glared at me.

"Get your dog away from my cat!" Tina yelled at Gregory. She was trying to coax Doofus Doolittle out of Mrs. Greene's garden. Casey had backed Doofus Doolittle into a corner. Doofus Doolittle was hissing and spitting. I had never seen him do anything like that before.

"This is your dumb sister's fault!"

Gregory said as he pulled his dog away from Doofus Doolittle.

"Don't call my sister dumb! Shut up before I hit you!" Tina said.

"Dumb! Dumb! Dumb!" Gregory said, looking in my direction.

Tina picked up Doofus Doolittle and without saying anything to anybody left the Greenes' backyard. I wondered if she was mad at me, too.

Pauline picked Tweetie's cage off the ground and dusted it off.

"Why did you do this, Willie?" she yelled at me as if she were blaming me for knocking Tweetie's cage on the ground. "If Mrs. Pyle finds out about it, she'll never let me watch Tweetie again." She looked like she was going to cry as she left the yard holding Tweetie's cage. Candy just looked at me and sighed. I could tell she felt sorry for me.

I climbed on the merry-go-round. I ran as fast as I could. When it was spinning fast I jumped on. I spun around faster and faster until everything was blurred. I closed my eyes and tried to pretend that nothing bad had happened. I hoped that everybody would be gone by the time the merry-go-round stopped. But there were still a couple of kids left when the merry-go-round finally stopped.

"Where is Boo?" Booker asked me. The last time I'd seen Boo was when Doofus Doolittle had chased him under the table. Had Doofus Doolittle really thought Boo was a mouse?

"I want Boo!" Booker said. Betty started to cry. Lena and Lana were still in the yard, too. They came over and Lena put her arm around Betty.

"We'll help you—"

"Find him," Lana said.

Lena took a carrot and a stalk of celery out of Boo's cage. Then she crawled under the table and looked around. Lana took tiny steps from the table into Mrs. Greene's garden. Then Lena spread chunks of carrot and celery near where Lana stood. They got down on the hands and knees and slowly crawled around the garden. They looked under the flowers and between the tomato plants. They looked between the rows of sunflowers that had been broken to the ground. They even looked under rocks. They put bits of carrot and celery everywhere. Lena put her fingers to her lips telling us to be very quiet. Then they sat on the ground and waited.

Soon Boo came out. He looked around very slowly. Then he rested on his hind legs. Lena held out a chunk of carrot, and he took it in his paws. Lena carefully picked him up and gave him to Booker.

"Boo!" Betty said very softy. She took him from her brother and gave him a kiss. She put him back in his cage with the other hamster. They left the Greenes' backyard smiling. That made me feel a little bit better.

Lena and Lana walked me home. They were the only kids on the block who were talking to me, the only ones who hadn't had pets in the show. When we got back to my house, we sat down on my back porch. I wasn't ready to face anybody yet, especially Tina. I didn't want to hear what she had to say. I was also afraid that Mrs. Greene had called Mrs. Cotton and told her what had happened, and that the whole thing had been my idea.

"Cheer up, Willie, it's not your fault," Lena said.

"Yes it is," I said.

"But you were just trying to earn some money," Lana said.

All I could do was sigh.

"We're really sorry," Lena and Lana said, both at the same time. Lena dropped her eyes. Lana dropped hers, too. I had never told them that I'd spent the cookie money on them, but I wondered if they had guessed.

"Can we—" Lena started.

"Do something to help?" Lena finished the sentence she had started.

"I can do tricks with my yo-yo," Lana said.

"I can read cards," Lena added.

I thought for a moment. "That's okay," I said. I was glad that they offered to help, but I wasn't up to any other moneymaking ideas. After the lemonade stand and the pet show, I didn't think I could take it.

When I went inside, Mrs. Cotton was setting the table for dinner. I knew my mother and father would be home soon. I wondered if Mrs. Greene would tell them about the pet show. I went to my room and closed the door. After a while, Tina came in.

"Are you mad at me, too?" I asked. "You can tell me the truth."

"Not mad, just embarrassed that you're my sister," Tina said. I knew I shouldn't have asked. Sometimes Tina didn't know when to stop. "But everybody else on the block is mad at you. Everybody wants their money back. Everybody. Even Lydia and Amber," she added.

"I feel terrible," I said. Tina pulled out the tin can with the money in it. "Want me to give it back for you?" she asked.

"Yeah," I said.

We sat there for a while, close to each other without saying anything.

"It was a good idea, Willie. It just didn't work out," she said. "Like the lemonade sale." She put her arm around me then, and we sat there on the bed for a while. It made me feel a little better, just sitting next to my sister like that. Maybe we were starting to live up to my father's nickname for us. Just in the nick of time.

Tina took the tin can and went back

outside to give everybody back their money. She asked if I wanted to help her, but I told her no. All I wanted to do was just sit there for a while. Although it wasn't my fault that everybody's pet had chased everybody else's, I wasn't ready to face anybody yet. I couldn't stop thinking about what had happened, especially the "what ifs."

What if one of the pets had gotten hurt? What if Doolittle had caught Boo or Casey had caught Doolittle? What if Snowflake had broken into Tweetie's cage and gobbled him down? What if Rusty had gotten Snowflake?

It was all because I was trying to earn some money because I hadn't told the truth about the cookie money.

I knew then what I had to do.

Setting Things Straight

Dear Mrs. Jones,

I wrote, and then I stopped writing. I thought about the other people who I hadn't told the complete truth to. I balled up that piece of paper and wrote a new greeting.

Dear Mrs. Jones, Mom, Dad, and the Girl Scouts of America,

I decided it would be better to write

three letters. I started again and wrote Mrs. Jones's letter first.

Dear Mrs. Jones,
I don't have the money that the people gave me for the Girl Scout cookies. I spent it all.

There! I had finally written it down in black and white. Actually, in green and white, since I'd borrowed Tina's colored pencils.

But Mrs. Jones and everybody else would want to know what I spent the money on, and so I wrote another line.

I spent the money on

I paused, unsure what to write next. I had promised Lena and Lana that I wouldn't tell anybody their secret. I had broken that promise when I told Tina. I didn't want to do it again, especially not in writing. On the other hand, I didn't want anybody to think that I'd spent all the money on myself. So I wrote:

a very worthy cause.

But a worthy cause could be anything, I realized. So I added:

Somebody on my street was hungry, and I bought them lunch for a week and a half. I'm very, very sorry that I spent the cookie money, but I'm not sorry that I bought the food for my friends. Here is ten dollars that my sister and I made selling lemonade. I promise that I will pay the rest back as soon as I can.

And then I added:

Somehow.

There didn't seem much else to say. So I finished my letter:

Sincerely,
Willimena T. Thomas
(Willie)

I read the letter three times to make sure it was okay. It said exactly what I wanted to say. I made two more copies, one for my mom and dad and one for the Girl Scouts, and put each in an envelope. Monday I would take Mrs. Jones her letter and the one for the Girl Scouts of America. I didn't want to think about what she would say or how she would feel. I just knew I had to face her and tell her the truth. Even if it was in a letter.

I had to face my parents, too. I placed

their letter on the bureau in their room. I leaned it up against the mirror so they would see it first thing when they came home. For a moment, I had second thoughts. But then I was happy it was done, even though I was still a little scared about what they would say. I knew they would be mad at me. But I also felt like I'd shoved a bear off the middle of my chest— a big, mean bear.

I was right about my parents being mad. They were really angry at me, even though they said I'd done the right thing in the wrong way. I had to pay back all the money from the savings account my father keeps for me at the bank. It was money I was saving to buy myself a GameBoy. But I felt good about giving the money back. Real good.

I was on punishment for a month, of course, and I couldn't watch TV for two weeks. So Tina watched whatever she wanted to watch and flipped the channels whenever she felt like it. She tried not to gloat, but I know my sister better than anybody else in the world, so she couldn't hide her true feelings from me. We will be the Sisters Umoja until the very end, I guess.

Even though I hadn't told them, my mom and dad guessed who the hungry kids on the block were. My mom stopped by to see Miss Wynn and invited Lena and Lana to spend the night whenever they wanted to. She also told Mrs. Cotton to make enough sandwiches for any kid who wanted to come for lunch at our house—even if it was the whole block.

Lena and Lana came practically every day after that, which was great for me. There was somebody else to tell Tina how yucky her tuna fish and ketchup sand-wiches were. But the best thing is that Lena and Lana won't be hungry anymore, and that made everything that had happened during the terrible week of the cookie money worth going through.

But I wouldn't want to go through it again.